A NOTE TO PARENTS

Disney's First Readers Level 3 books were developed for children who have mastered many basic reading skills and are on the road to becoming competent and confident readers.

Disney's First Readers Level 3 books have more fully developed plots, introduce harder words, and use more complex sentence and paragraph structures than Level 2 books.

Reading is the single most important way a young person learns to enjoy reading. Give your child opportunities to read many different types of literature. Make books, magazines, and writing materials available to your child. Books that are of special interest to your child will motivate more reading and provide more enjoyment. Here are some additional tips to help you spend quality reading time with your child:

★ Promote thinking skills. Ask if your child liked the story or not and why. This is one of the best ways to learn if your child understood what he or she has read.

★ Continue to read aloud. No matter how old the child may be, or how proficient a reader, hearing a delightful story read aloud is still exciting and a very important part of becoming a more fluent reader.

★ Read together on a regular basis, and encourage your child to read to you often. Be a good teacher by being a good listener and audience!

★ Praise all reading efforts, no matter how small.

★ Try out the After-Reading Fun activities at the end of each book to enhance the skills your child has already learned.

Remember that early-reading experiences that you share with your child can help him or her to become a confident and successful reader later on!

— Patricia Koppman
Past President
International Reading Association

First published by Random House, Inc., New York, New York.
This edition published by Scholastic Inc.,
90 Old Sherman Turnpike, Danbury, Connecticut 06816
by arrangement with Disney Licensed Publishing.

SCHOLASTIC and associated logos are trademarks of Scholastic Inc.

ISBN 0-7172-6658-3

Printed in the U.S.A.

DISNEY·PIXAR
MONSTERS, INC.

Boo on the Loose

by Gail Herman
Illustrated by Scott Tilley, Floyd Norman,
and Brooks Campbell

Disney's First Readers — Level 3
A Story from Disney/Pixar's *Monsters, Inc.*

★★★

SCHOLASTIC INC.
New York Toronto London Auckland Sydney
Mexico City New Delhi Hong Kong Buenos Aires

James P. Sullivan, or Sulley, was the top Scarer at Monsters, Inc. He was Scarer of the Month more times than anyone else. Scaring kids and collecting their screams was a very important job. Kids' screams powered the whole city of Monstropolis.

Sulley worked on the Scare Floor.
When a child's door was in place,
Sulley waited for the signal. The red
light meant he could open the door . . .

. . . and scare the kid on the other side.
Monsters, Inc. turned the screams into
energy. Big scares meant big screams.
And big screams meant big energy!

One night, Sulley was heading home. He walked past the Scare Floor and saw a door still set up. All the doors should have been put away in the door vault.

"Is anybody scaring in here?" Sulley whispered, peeking inside the room.

Sulley turned around to find a KID clinging to his tail.

"Boo!" it said. It was a little girl— and she was inside the monster world!

"Aaaah!"
Sulley screamed.

Every monster believed that children were dangerous. They were like poison to monsters. So Sulley carefully tried to carry the kid back into her room.

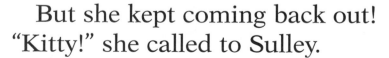

But she kept coming back out!
"Kitty!" she called to Sulley.

Sulley had to do something. If anyone found out there was a kid loose in Monstropolis, who knew what would happen?!

There was only one monster
Sulley could tell his secret to—his
best friend, Mike. He was sure
that Mike would know what to do.
So Sulley sneaked the little girl
out in a bag and took her home.

Mike couldn't believe it! A kid? In
Monstropolis? In their own home?

"Sulley, it can't stay here!" Mike declared.

"Her name is Boo," said Sulley.

"You *named* it already?" cried Mike.

They had to get rid of the kid—and
fast! Mike came up with a plan. The
next morning, they would drive her to
the park and try to lose her.

While she was sleeping, Sulley and Mike peeked in on Boo.

"Hey! Wait a minute!" said Mike. "That's *my* bear!"

"Shhh! You can have him back tomorrow," Sulley told him.

The next morning, Sulley and Mike disguised Boo in a monster costume they had made. Then they walked outside to Mike's car.

"Be careful," warned Mike. "Don't let that kid touch anything!"

When they got to the park, Sulley and Mike got out of the car. Mike went to open the door for Boo, but she had locked herself in!

Mike was *not* happy. "We have to get her out!" he said. "NOW!"

Sulley thought for a moment. Then he came up with an idea . . .

Sulley put Mike in the middle of the spare tire. He rolled Mike all around. "Isn't this fun?" Sulley said.

"Yeah, real fun," Mike grumbled.

Boo smiled, but she didn't get out of the car.

So Sulley grabbed Mike by the arms and swung him around and around. "Don't you want to play, Boo?" he called.

Mike was hoping that this time it would work. He was getting very, very dizzy! But Boo stayed in the car.

Just then a monster butterfly flew past the car window. Boo was fascinated as she smiled and pointed at it. Then she opened the car door and ran after it!

Boo followed the butterfly into the park. She tried to catch it, but the butterfly was too fast. Up, up, up it went . . .

. . . and then it flew right into the woods! Boo giggled as she continued to chase after it.

Mike grabbed Sulley's arm. "Now's our chance, Sulley!" shouted Mike. "The kid's gone! Let's go!"

Mike tried to start the engine. But the car wouldn't start.

"Oh, great," sighed Mike. "We're out of fuel! Just our luck!"

But Sulley wasn't listening. He was thinking about Boo and realized that he missed her already. Who was going to call him "Kitty" now?

Then Sulley had a super sneaky idea! If Mike thought that they *needed* Boo, Sulley could go after her and get her back.

"We need to find Boo," Sulley said to Mike. "Her scream will start the car!"

Without waiting for Mike's
answer, Sulley ran into the woods.
"Boo?" Sulley called. "I have your
teddy bear . . . "

But Sulley didn't see her anywhere.
"Boo, where are you?" he called. "Boo?"
Oh, no! Where could she be?

"Kitty?" said a small voice.

"Boo!" cried Sulley. He was happier than he could ever remember as Boo ran right to him. She gave him a hug. Now Sulley was sure: Boo wasn't dangerous at all.

Sulley and Boo happily walked back to the car.

Mike couldn't believe what he was seeing. "Are you crazy? You're holding its hand!" Mike cried.

Sulley just smiled. "I know," he said.
"I feel okay, though."

Sulley smiled as he put Boo
back in the car.

"Now we need some scream," said Mike. "Sulley, you are the best Scarer at Monsters, Inc. Do your stuff!"

Sulley turned around and looked
at Boo. She smiled back at him. He
opened his mouth to roar . . . but he
just couldn't do it. He just couldn't
scare little Boo!

Mike gripped the steering wheel in frustration. "Just scare it, NOW!" he yelled. He banged his head on the steering wheel.

HONK! went the horn.

"Ouch!" cried Mike.

Boo giggled. "Hee-hee-hee!"

Just then the engine started with a roar! Mike and Sulley looked at each other. Whoa! How did that happen?

Mike looked at Boo. "All right, okay, she can stay—for now," he said.

"But just remember," added Mike, "that's *my* bear!"

Enhance the reading experience with follow-up questions to help your child develop reading comprehension and increase his/her awareness of words.

Approach this with a sense of play. Make a game of having your child answer the questions. You do not need to ask all the questions at one time. Let these questions be fun discussions rather than a test. If your child doesn't have instant recall, encourage him/her to look back into the book to "research" the answers. You'll be modeling what good readers do and, at the same time, forging a sharing bond with your child.

Boo on the Loose

1. **What does Boo call Sulley?**

2. **How did Mike and Sulley disguise Boo?**

3. **What did Boo follow into the woods?**

4. **Have you ever shared one of your toys with someone else? How did it make you feel?**

5. **How did the car finally start?**

6. **What words can you make from** *Monstropolis?*

Answers: 1. Kitty. 2. they dressed her up as a little monster. 3. a monster butterfly. 4. answers will vary. 5. Boo's laughter made the energy to start the car. 6. *possible answers:* on, is, in, son, ton, pot, lot, slot, stop, top, mop, slip, slit, stir, slim, troop, soon, moon, spoon, sit.